Margot

Kevin Stewart

—Winner: *Texas Review* Novella Prize for 1999—

Printed in the United States of America

FIRST EDITION, 2000

Permissions
Texas Review Press
English Department
Sam Houston State University
Huntsville, TX 77341-2146

Cover photography by Kevin Stewart

Library of Congress Cataloging-in-Publication Data

Stewart, Kevin, 1962-
Margot / Kevin Stewart.-- 1st ed.
p. cm.
ISBN 1-881515-29-X
1. Title.

PS3569.T465256 M3 2000
813'.6--dc21

00-062017

Margot

Margot

The weekend after Thanksgiving, my partner Harris and I were remodeling the cabins of the Buffalo River Tourist Court in Jasper, Arkansas, one of those old spreads that reminded me of the roadsides along Route 66 in *The Grapes of Wrath.* The identical cabins were log, stained dark as railroad ties, with chinking discolored by weather and mildew. Inside, the walls were covered with old v-notch knotty pine. Real paneling—interlocking three-quarter-inch tongue-and-groove pieces of various widths—not the sheets of fake crap you buy at the builders' supply store.

She was in number five. I accidentally walked in on her, thinking I was heading into number four, which we'd been working on. The door was unlocked. My tool belt around my waist, I carried a crowbar in one hand, a stepladder in the other. That day we were to begin tearing out the ceiling tiles and replacing them with sheets of bead board to make the units look more authentically 1920's.

When the light from the open door fell across her, she quickly sat up, shielding her eyes with one arm. "What the—" she said. Her other arm was holding the sheet over her chest. "Who are you?"

"Sorry," I said.

Pulling the sheet up to her neck, she squinted her eyes at me in the glare of the morning light.

"I'm remodeling the place," I said.

"Now?"

"Well, not this specific one," I said. Her hair was dark and reddish, the color of stained cherry, done up in some kind of do but disheveled from sleep. She looked a little younger than I was, but not by much—thirty-nine, forty. She was short, no more than five feet tall, I could tell, even though she was hidden under blankets. I have an eye for proportions, for lengths and distances. She had curves, though, rolling, under that sheet. Backing out, I said, "Came in the wrong one. Sorry."

She watched me, still too bewildered and not yet awake enough to decide whether to be angry or scared. "Be more careful," she said.

"You should lock the door." On the stoop now, I closed the door. I noticed her gold Saturn sedan, with temporary Texas tags and a dealer sticker from Fort Worth, was parked between numbers five and six, pulled in as far as it would go. From where my truck was parked, I hadn't seen it and wasn't expecting anyone to be staying in any cabin except number six—bow hunters from Missouri. The Buffalo National River runs near here. Public hunting, fishing, and canoeing. The peak tourist season is March and early April, when the water's up from spring run-off. Then, the river is like a railroad track, trains of canoes floating it. The outfitters, stores, motels, and campgrounds all make their money over that five or six week period. By the end of May, though, the river is too low to float. Except for horseback riders and hikers, you have the stream to yourself. It's peaceful. The cliffs dwarf you. And the water is full of smallmouth bass the color of new pennies. In the fall, the hunters take over.

"Over here," Harris said. He was standing on the stoop of number four wearing his old Army field jacket he'd had since Vietnam. He grinned like he had seen the Saturn and known all along that someone was in the room.

I headed toward him. "Why didn't you tell me?"

He laughed, then disappeared inside.

An hour later, my circular saw was screaming. An eighteen-inch section of bead board fell to the ground. I shut the saw off, and fresh-cut pine smell was whipped away by the breeze. It was a little warm for early December, in the fifties, but it was cloudy and windy. A front was coming down out of Kansas and Missouri, coming to chill things. You could tell by the clacking of the bare tree limbs on the mountains, the roar in the pines.

"Is there a good breakfast near here?" she asked, startling me a bit, and I turned around.

She'd seen me flinch. "We're even," she said. Smiling, she wore jeans and an unzipped, too-heavy emerald parka. Her hair was fixed now, but I didn't like its exaggerations, the stiff waves, and there were hints of gray. She didn't wear much make-up. But those were my only complaints, and I was right about her height.

"Across the bridge," I said. "The Ozark Inn."

"Within walking distance?"

"Not more than a hundred yards."

In number four, Harris yanked furring strips from the ceiling, the nails crying in the fork of his claw hammer.

"Good coffee?"

"Espresso, cappuccino, gourmet. A lot of yuppies come here from Kansas City, Memphis, Dallas," I said, then glanced at her car. "That where you're from?"

"Are you saying I'm a yuppie?"

Face flushing, I thought I'd insulted her and started to apologize. She smiled and said, "I'm from Fort Worth."

"Where abouts?" I said. "I've been down that way a few times."

"Oh, one of those old suburbs." Her smile flattening, she gazed at the mountains that surrounded town. "You know how they're all alike," she said. "Unlike mountains." She removed her hands from her coat pockets, put on a pair of horned-rimmed sunglasses. There was no wedding band. There was hardly any jewelry at all on her. In her right ear was a diamond stud no larger than the head of a ten-penny nail. A thin pink scar ran from the stud to the bottom of her lobe, like maybe an earring had been yanked out.

"Well, the Ozark Inn'll get you off to a good start this morning," I said.

"I'm a little more interested in stopping," she said and headed toward the bridge. I watched her walk away and wished that bulky parka wasn't hiding her form.

All was not well in Newton County. Elk were being killed along the Buffalo River. Twenty years ago, thirty elk were reintroduced to the river, transplanted from the Rockies, and a number of them died during a wintertime disease epidemic. Others were poached until the locals, from Boxley Hollow to the river's confluence with the White River, did a sort of neighborhood watch. The elk would ease into the field at dusk, easy targets for road hunters with spotlights. A gun shot, and the nearest neighbors raced to the scene and caught men dragging an elk back to their truck. The locals would get the license numbers and turn the men in. The law came down hard on them: jail time, confiscation of firearms, and huge fines, and the poaching stopped. Soon the elk resisted the disease. They were common all along the river now. DNR estimate was 170 animals. There was talk of opening an official limited hunting season.

Now, someone else was killing them, and this time it was worse.

They weren't killing the animals for meat or even trophies. They were just leaving the elk lying dead. And they were not shooting from the road. They were riding dirt bikes and four-wheelers down the horse paths, miles from the access points. Horseback riders and legitimate hunters had found a dozen dead elk this month—bulls and cows.

And it was a shame, because this time of year, the elk are great. Mating season. At Ponca, people line the roadside and watch the animals in the fields. A bull elk's whistle is a sound you never forget. It cuts the chilled air like a warning signal. The bulls spar, locking antlers. And they're not shy about mounting a cow before a large human audience, and you're not sure whether you're seeing something you shouldn't see.

Saturday was my night to join my neighbor, Milton Panas, on horses and ride the trail from Jasper to Kyle's Landing. Milton had reestablished the "neighborhood watch," but, in our case, the neighborhood was thousands of acres of Ozark Mountain wilderness. We were volunteer informants on civilian patrol and rode the trails along the river once a week listening for shots, for motorcycle and four-wheeler engines, trying to catch the killers. But they were hard to detect. They knew the river, and they used crossbows and compound bows. And the elk, not used to hunting pressure, weren't shy of humans. You could walk right up to them.

Milton owned the horses. I was no expert horseman, but his animals were gentle, well-broken. He'd named all of them, even mares, after characters John Wayne had played. He said there were no more John Waynes, but I argued he was only an actor. He said I knew what he meant. He rode Cahill. I rode Jack Cutter. We had food, water, First Aid kits, and emergency flares in our saddlebags. He carried a walkie-talkie. We had shotguns in scabbards fastened to the saddles.

That night was more December-like than the past few days had been. There was very little moon, a half coffee cup ring. The limestone bluffs towering over the river cast their own illumination, the river washing along the base of them. Slack water lay against the opposite bank, where the valley gradually eased into the water. The trail crossed the river every mile or so.

"The killers been coming in off private land," Milton said, riding Cahill ahead of me.

"Somebody's gotta be letting them," I said.

We ducked under a low-hanging branch, holding our hats. The

hooves of the horses were muffled in the sandy river-bottom soil.

"If it ain't somebody that owns land along the park," he said. "A lot of people are still mad about the government coming in and taking land like they did."

"Eminent domain," I said.

"Imminent trouble," he said. "But you can't blame nobody for getting mad about losing their land. Some of these places had been in people's families since way back before the Civil War."

We passed the shell of an abandoned barn, the stone foundation of a house. Houses, barns, and outbuildings, abandoned in the early seventies, were scattered all along the river. Broken down fences and rotted posts lined much of its banks. The horse trails were once roads to people's houses.

Two hours later, we were easing along the river. Occasional coyotes howled from atop the bluffs, rabbits darted this way and that, the flags of white tail deer blurred into the woods. Milton shone his flashlight on a set of dirt bike tire tracks, curving from an old logging road onto the horse path.

"Looks awful fresh," he said.

"We'd heard it," I said. In this canyon, with the air cold and still like it was, you could hear a motor for miles. "Probably from last night."

He nodded, staring at the logging road. "Let's follow it into the woods," he said. "Might be where they're coming in."

Where it forked from the river bottom, the road was grown up with bamboo, then with locust saplings and cedars to the base of the mountain, where the woods began. The road zigzagged the slope, cut through a gap in the rocks at a forty-five degree angle, then topped the ridge. Below us, the river horseshoed around the foot of the mountain. The motorcycle tracks continued along the ridge-top in the opposite direction of the river. We followed. A couple hundred yards later we came upon another old barn, which appeared to be in pretty good shape.

As we approached the door, we caught a whiff of diesel fuel and an acrid chemical smell I couldn't place. The horses flinched at the fumes. "Easy does it, Cahill," Milton said. We dismounted, tied the horses off to an old fence post and went to the barn.

Milton shone his light inside. Scattered on the floor were dozens of empty anti-freeze jugs and hundreds of opened allergy medicine boxes and foil-backed plastic packages, the pills pushed through the foil. There were Drano cans and what looked to be thousands of kitchen matches with the heads pinched off. A glob of amber, stiff as pinesap and enough to fill a fifty-five gallon drum, lay in the corner.

"I seen this on the news," Milton said.

"The hell is it?"

"Unless I'm wrong," he said, "it's a meth lab."

"Methamphetamine?"

"Looks like it," he said. "Redneck crack. Hell, Hitler even made the German soldiers take it during the war to keep them awake, to make them fight without giving a damn about their own selves."

I studied the glob a moment, then followed Milton back to the horses. He called the ranger's office on the walkie-talkie and told them what we'd found.

"Wanna keep following the tracks?" he asked.

"We're after elk killers, aren't we?"

He scanned the woods. "I reckon you're right."

We rode back down the mountainside and followed the river back to Route 7, neither of us saying much. The wind picked up. The first traces of clouds drifted over the mouth of the canyon. The meth lab worried me. I'd moved out here because of the serenity, the peace and quiet that comes with nature. Nothing was safe anymore.

When I first moved here, after my divorce, everyone seemed a little leery of me. I wanted to do something to try to fit in and was thankful when Milton called one day and asked for my help. One thing people do here is help each other. You help your neighbor because one day you might need his help. Milton owned a turkey farm. Last summer the temperature rose above a hundred every day for two weeks, and his damn turkeys were cooking alive, dying of heat prostration. Milton had hoped he could wait the heat wave out, but the weatherman had forecast at least another week of it. He called me up, asked if I'd help him get rid of some dead turkeys. I was thinking maybe a few dozen or something, so I showed up.

Milton was waiting with what looked like a hundred boxes of shells and a couple of .22 magnum rifles. At least half the turkeys were dead in every one of the barns. Panting, eyes half-covered with blue lids, the rest were barely hanging on. We started shooting. An hour later, ears ringing, the air stinking of gunpowder, turkey shit, and raw poultry, I staggered outside to keep the stench from gagging me and saw there was one turkey left, a gobbler. He'd escaped a barn, made it out to the middle of the field. He looked healthy. I put the cross hairs on him, but Milton said, "Hold it. I'll keep thatun. He looks like a survivor."

As we scooped up turkey carcasses with a front-end loader to haul to the landfill, that turkey pecked around in the middle of the field. Milton kept him and treated him like a dog.

After our patrol along the river, I slept most of Sunday. It was almost dark by the time I'd gotten up and, in the rain, hauled in a rick of firewood for my wood stove. That cold wouldn't be long following the rain.

I showered, left my house on Parthenon Road and went to Jasper for something to eat, like I often did. Hanging around the house alone made me feel uneasy. An architect friend from college designed the house for my ex-wife, Patricia, and me. But she left me with the prints and no house. I decided to build it anyway, only out in the country rather than in that new development in Goshen. No use letting a nice design go to waste. But the house is big and it has Patricia's mark on it—the rooms she wanted, like a sitting room, a study; and a big master-bath with a double vanity, refurbished clawfoot bath tub, and glass block shower stall. Those spaces still seem like hers even though she's never set foot in the place and even though I've hung gun and fishing rod racks on the walls in them and put a pool table in the sitting room.

Driving past the Buffalo River Tourist Court, I looked to see if the Saturn was still there. It was. The window of the cabin was yellow with light. I thought about stopping, inviting her to dinner, but I convinced myself she wasn't interested, that she was just passing. I drove on. Along the short Main Street and around the courthouse square, Christmas decorations had been attached to the streetlight poles—alternating snowmen and candy canes.

Inside the Ozark Inn, I saw her at a booth, by herself, smoking, reading a book. A coffee cup steamed near the book.

I walked over, said, "Boo."

She jumped slightly.

"One up on you again," I said.

"Paybacks are hell," she said, smiling at me. "Here alone?"

"Yep." I sat down, inferring an invitation. "Good book?"

"Found it at the indoor rummage sale on the square," she said. It's about a football player, but it's all over the place. This guy wouldn't know a plot if it hit him in the a—" She paused, then said, "Face."

"Don't hold back on my account," I said. "My ears aren't virgin."

She ground out the cigarette. "Well, I wouldn't wanna give a bad impression."

"Looking to impress somebody?"

"You never know," she said, laying the book facedown on the wood grain of the table.

I picked up the book, hefted it—the weight of a brick—and set it down. I recognized the writer—a guy who taught over at the university. "You just come here to read, or did you eat?"

"I ate," she said, "but I don't mind watching." She sipped coffee, then took out another cigarette. "Mind if I smoke?"

Though I did, I said, "Not at all," and grabbed a menu from behind the napkin dispenser. The waitress came, took my order, brought me coffee too.

I raised my cup to the woman across the booth from me, a woman whose name I didn't know, and I said, "Here's to chance meetings."

She clinked her cup against mine. "To chance meetings."

"By the way, let me introduce myself. I'm Frank," I said. "Frank Powell."

She cleared her throat. "Margot," she said. "Margot Bailey."

We shook hands, hers as soft and smooth as a silk scarf. Her eyes were the green color of tarnished copper flashing. Her cheeks were a little hollow, but delicate. She had almost imperceptible crow's-feet. The skin under her chin sagged only slightly. She was aging with grace.

We talked as I ate, mostly about me. "You always lived here?" she asked.

"Only for a couple of years now," I said. "I'm from over near Fayetteville."

"Where's that from here?" She lit another cigarette.

"Didn't you come through there to get here?"

"I wasn't paying any attention."

"It's west of here," I said. "About ninety minutes."

"No tourist courts to remodel over there?"

"No, well, I was an engineer for the city sewage treatment plant," I said. "I removed the sh—well, you've heard of shit jobs."

"Yours was literal."

I took a sip of coffee, lowered my voice a notch. "And in the meantime, my ex-wife decided it wasn't very glamorous either."

"Was she a little uppity?"

"Not at first."

"Kids?"

"Two girls," I said. "Sarah and Rhiannon."

"Fleetwood Mac fans, huh?"

"Well, she was," I said. "I see the girls every couple of weeks—once a month out here. A friend of mine has horses he lets them ride. The girls like the country."

"They take after you, I guess."

"Proud to say it looks like it." Over the loudspeakers, dogs barked "Jingle Bells." I looked at the mount of a twelve-point buck on the wall adjacent to us. A Santa's hat was on its head. Christmas bulbs dangled from the antlers. A red ball was stuck on its nose. Patricia would cringe, but Margot seemed to settle right in.

"So what's your ex do that's so prestigious?" she asked.

"Works for Wal-Mart."

"And she dumped you?"

I laughed. "Well, she's an MBA. Washington University in St. Louis, a rich kids' school. Works at Wal-Mart's corporate office in Bentonville."

She looked me over for a moment. "You must've married late."

"Thirty-one," I said. "Figured by then I'd be mature enough to handle it."

"And you weren't?"

"I don't know," I said. "She changed—the higher up Wal-Mart's ladder she climbed, the less appealing me and my job looked."

"So Wal-Mart's headquartered around here?"

"Yep," I said. "Being from Texas, you probably already knew that."

"Well," she said, "We've got our own millionaires to worry about."

"You don't sound like you're from Texas," I said.

She glanced away and swayed a little to a Muzak version of "White Christmas." "I grew up in Tennessee," she said, flicking ashes into the tray. "When I was in junior high school, my daddy moved us to Texas to find work."

"That happens around here too, like Dallas is paradise."

"I had all I could stand of it."

After a pause, I asked, "How long are you in town?"

"I don't know," she said. "Seemed like a good isolated place to get away from everything for a while."

"Everything?"

She finished off her coffee, took another drag from her cigarette. "It's a long story."

"The new car and all?"

"Yeah." She ground out the cigarette. "Well, Mr. Powell," she said, "I should get back to my little cabin even though I feel like I'm in solitary confinement in that thing."

I wanted to tell her I had a large three-bedroom house all to myself, but I took a business card from my wallet instead, handed it to her, something I didn't often do in non-business situation. "Ever need anything," I said, "give me a call."

She took it, looked at it, slipped it into her purse. "I will," she said. She slid from the booth, put on her parka, tucked the book under her arm and left. I ordered another cup of coffee and a slice of peach pie.

On the way home, I looked at the yellow square of light in number five. A car horn blew in front of me. I jerked the wheel and whipped back onto my side of the double line.

One thing about Jasper, there are no women. Sometimes, I'd go to Eureka Springs, an old turn-of-the-century resort town and the closest "wet" town to Jasper. I liked to stay in the historic hotel rooms, drink in the old bars that were speakeasies in the 20's. A couple of times, I shared the experience with a companion. Or when I went to Fayetteville to visit the kids, I'd get a room and go out after taking the girls home. Met an older graduate student once, a city girl from the coast, and gave her my card too. Afterward, she kept calling me. She didn't understand those encounters were short-term, and when you've spent the better part of eight years with a woman, five of them married, you know the difference between the short-term and commitment, which is what you think you really want, and you think you know it when you meet someone you'd like to be with for a while. For a long time, I didn't know if another chance would come. Thinking of Margot, I smiled.

The next day, Milton stopped by the tourist court as Harris and I unloaded a plastic shower stall from the back of my truck.

"There was another one last night," he said.

"Elk?" I said.

"Near the Boy Scout camp. A cow," Milton said. "Just left it laying there."

"Bastards," Harris said. "Those elk ain't hurting nobody."

We carried the stall inside the cabin, set it down on the bathroom floor. Milton watched from the stoop, bundled in his fur-lined denim coat. He had on a plaid wool hat with earflaps. "Now we got them meth labs to worry about too," he said.

"Meth labs?" Harris said. "Here?"

"Looks like it," I said.

"Rangers are out searching the old barns and whatnot along the river for more," Milton said. "They got a Haz-Mat team cleaning up the one we found. And a bomb squad detonating boobytraps."

"Boobytraps?" I said.

"Yep," Milton said. "Homemade land mines. If it ain't one sort of meanness, it's another."

"Well, at least you know why they're making meth," I said. "For money. But why are the elk getting killed?"

"Like Milton said," Harris said. "Meanness."

"You riding with me again Saturday night?" Milton asked me.

"Why wouldn't I?" I asked, heading back outside.

"Thought you'd think twice after hearing about them mines."

"It does add a new element," I said. "But I'll still go along, I guess."

"You wanna come, Harris?" Milton asked. "Got plenty of horses. You could ride McClintock."

"Old lady wouldn't like it much," Harris said. "She likes for me to watch the baby on weekends so she can see her sisters."

"Well," Milton said. "You're welcome anytime."

"From what I heard about meth, the way it fucks people up, I don't know if I'd go down there anyways," Harris said. "Makes people hyper. Paranoid. Trigger happy."

"Really?" I said.

"You gonna chicken out now?" Milton asked me.

"No, but this—"

"We're just acting like eyes," he said. "We see something, we call the rangers." He walked back to his truck, still going on about the elk. He pulled out, blew his horn. As he drove away we waved at his dented and horse shit-stained tailgate, the wooden cattle racks rattling on the bed of the truck.

Heading back inside number four, I stopped at the doorway, saw Margot leave her room and get in her car. I wondered if she was checking out, but she had no luggage with her and didn't stop to drop off the key. She pulled out of the parking lot, headed west out of town.

"Nice looking lady, ain't she?" Harris asked. I glanced at his thin face, razor stubble turning a little white, grinning at me.

"Not bad at all," I said.

"Why you reckon she's here?"

"I've been wondering that myself," I said. "She's hard to pin down."

"You tried, did you?"

I faked a right at him, gave him a finger punch in the gut with my left, and he mimed a combination. "Let's get that commode inside," I said.

"Get your mind out of it first," he said. "Won't be so heavy thataway."

I'd hired Harris back in the summer, after I'd gone through three men who didn't know which end of the nail to hit, but those were the only kind who'd risk working for a new contractor like me. Till Harris showed up. One day he just walked out of his job at the Tyson plant in Berryville. Couldn't take anymore. I couldn't blame him. I wouldn't wish forty hours a week of eviscerating chickens on anyone. He'd been in Vietnam. He had a wife, his third, and a fifteen-month-old kid. He had four other kids from his other two marriages. Up front, he told me he'd been arrested once, back in the 70's for farming pot over in Madison County, but he'd been clean ever since. I believed him because he worked hard.

Before I left work that evening, and after not seeing Margot come back, I stopped by the tourist court office. The owner said she hadn't checked out. Her things were still in her room when they'd cleaned it. "Do you know her?" she asked.

"I'm getting there," I said.

At home, after a shower and a frozen pizza, I'd almost called her room several times but didn't. I convinced myself she wasn't back yet or that she'd returned and left. She was no more attractive than anyone else I'd dated, or married, but she wore mystery the way some women wear just the right kind and right amount of fragrance. I liked her easy-going ways, just enough refinement, just enough of a raw edge. Unlike in Patricia, I could see a little of myself in Margot, something to connect with. We'd both run from something and ended up here. But I was still nervous. Even when something seems like fate, you can't help but doubt yourself, to think you're making something out of nothing.

I started to call again, but the plate, fork, and beer glass I'd just dirtied needed cleaning. I sat them in the sink, turned on the faucet, and the phone rang. I shut the water off, answered it.

"Is this Powell's Construction and Remodeling?"

It was her. Her voice tried to feign business, but it was a little slurred, as if she'd been drinking. Sweat moistened my hand that gripped the receiver. "Yes, ma'am, it is," I said, playing along.

"What's your reputation, I mean, as a remodeler?"

"I do the best work around, ask anybody."

"Can you make a sober lady drunk?" she asked, sounding more country than she had before. "Cause, honey, there ain't a drink to be found in this town."

"It's dry as a librarian's sense of humor," I said. "But I'm not. Got a fifth of Maker's Mark with the wax still unbroken."

"Sounds like you're the man for the job."

I switched the receiver to my other hand, wiped my right palm on the leg of my pants. "I'll be right there," I said.

"I'd rather come there," she said. "Too cramped here. I'm going stir crazy."

"We can fix that too," I said. "I got all the room you need."

"I need all I can get."

I gave her directions, changed shirts three times until I found one, a sky blue Oxford, that was less wrinkled than the others. I swabbed a couple of highball glasses to clean off the dishwasher spots and the dust. The matching highball, beer, wine, and champagne glasses in the liquor cabinet were Patricia's idea. She liked to host dinner parties for her Wal-Mart cronies, but she left me with the glasses. Why, I don't know. I normally drink from whatever glasses are handy. Until now, those glasses in the cabinet hadn't been touched since I'd put them there when I moved in.

Patricia and I came from two different worlds. My family owned a farm west of Fayetteville, near Lincoln. And my dad was a signal maintainer for the Arkansas/Missouri Railroad, a small line that runs from Joplin to Fort Smith. My family had always made out fine, but they kept things simple. Meals were necessary parts of the day, like feeding the cattle or weeding the garden.

Patricia's family, though, was not quite the same. Her folks were both professionals in St. Louis. They had cocktails before dinner. They used salad bowls instead of putting salad on the dinner plate. They laid their butter knives across the edge of small bread plates that held rolls or slices of French bread. They set out a water glass and another glass for wine, ice tea, or whatever. They used napkins, not paper towels, and they laid them across their laps.

Margot's car turning into the driveway set the dogs off. From the front door, I called them off, sent them around back. She climbed out of her car, wearing a long black coat, not the parka. Her hair was different, darker, flatter, straighter, but not much shorter. Below the hem of her coat were thin ankles covered with dark sheer hose. She wore low-heeled, black pumps. Had I just gotten a glance of her on the street, I don't know that I'd have recognized her. I held the door open and she walked inside, a light fragrance of rose following her in. I took her coat. She had on a knee-length black dress, the neckline plunging between her shoulder blades. On her pale skin there was fine peach fuzz. I told her to have a seat, hung her coat in the foyer closet.

"Nice place," she said, looking around. "I like the cathedral ceiling. The wood. It feels warm."

"Thanks," I said. "An architect friend I went to school with designed it."

"No Christmas tree?"

"Haven't been feeling too Christmassy."

"Stone hearth. Wood stove. No fireplace? You can't hang stockings above a wood stove."

"Decided on the stove instead," I said. "More efficient. If I'm gonna cut and split wood, I want heat from it. Santa'll have to use the front door."

"A bit of a Scrooge, aren't you?"

"Disappointed?"

"Well," she said. "Bourbon and fireplaces do go hand-in-hand."

"One out of two's not bad."

She smiled. "I guess not."

I asked her how she liked her bourbon.

"On the rocks with just a kiss of club soda."

I mixed it, handed it to her with a bar napkin. She downed it in one gulp, gave the glass back to me before I could even turn to go to my chair. I examined it a moment. She drank like someone who needed to.

As I mixed another, I said, "Awfully dressed up tonight."

"Went shopping today," she said. "I have very few things with me. Found an outlet mall in Branson."

"Branson?"

She laughed. "Quite a place, Branson."

"You probably lowered the average age by twenty years."

"It was actually a little dead," she said. "I did luck into one place that served drinks."

"Wait till spring," I said.

"Expecting me to hang around that long?"

I carried her new drink to her. "I hope so."

She took it, watching me, her smile cocked into a smirk. "To spring," she said.

We clinked glasses, downed the drinks.

"So, why are you here?" I asked.

She set her glass on the coffee table. "I guess it would cause you to wonder after a while."

"It does make me wonder—an attractive woman. New car. You just show up here."

"In Jasper?"

"In Jasper, of all places."

She took out a cigarette, nodded at it. "All right?"

I got an ashtray from the bar, placed it beside her empty glass, then grabbed her glass.

"Another?"

"You bet."

After she finished the third drink, she started talking, choosing words like a good framer chooses a wall stud, eyeing for straightness and trueness. Until then, though, getting a story out of her was harder than extracting a wood-screw with a claw hammer.

"My husband was killed," she said. "We were robbed coming in the back door of the house from the garage." She paused, took a drag from her cigarette, blew smoke. "The garage was detached from the house," she said. "Funny, the designer said it was safer that way.

"They came from the alley, two of them. They had Halloween masks on. Two of the Seven Dwarfs. That struck me as so strange I forgot what was going on for a moment, until they demanded Arnold's wallet, my purse, our jewelry. But Arnold was always easy to rile. He was a loudmouth too, liked to argue. One of the things I liked about him was he hated to lose an argument. At parties, I've seen him make whole rooms uneasy by arguing with someone. I never liked those parties. Businessmen, accountants. Money money everywhere."

"I know what you mean. Except I got left behind for those things."

"Feel fortunate," she said.

"I do," I said. "Now."

She looked at me. "That bottle run dry, or does this place have a three-drink maximum?"

I made her another drink, glad she was talking, whether her story was true or not. She sipped this glass, then rested it on her thigh, legs crossed, the hem of her dress tight across her knees.

"Where was I?" she asked.

"The robbers," I said, still on my second drink.

"They demanded our things," she said. "Arnold told them to fuck off." She paused, took another sip. "Grumpy shot him," she said. "It was so loud. I stood there, staring at Sneezy, with my husband writhing on the ground for a few moments before he died. Sneezy pointed his gun at me. I begged him not to kill me." She looked across the room, at a framed rendering of Old Main, the oldest building on the University of Arkansas campus.

"Grumpy went through Arnold's pockets, stripped off his Rolex, his wedding band, tie clip. Anything hard and shiny, they took it. Then he took my jewelry, my purse, yanked the earrings from my lobes, and told me to lie down. The earrings left scars."

"I noticed that," I said. "That must've hurt."

"I didn't feel it."

She took another drink, kept her eyes trained on the glass. "I lay down on the brick patio, crying, because I knew I was going to die beside a man I didn't love anymore, and everyone would think that we'd died together. Some romantic b.s. like that. I was only there because I didn't have the guts to leave him. I've never worked. A degree in education and I've never used it. I lived off his money." She stopped again, downed the rest of the bourbon.

"Obviously they didn't shoot you."

"Obviously not." She held her glass out to me, nodded at it. I finished mine, took them both back to the bar. As I refilled them, she lit another cigarette, then settled back into the couch. She appeared to be finished.

As she'd told her story, I began to believe it was true, but I wondered why it seemed so calculated, so cold. I liked her a little less then, but I told myself that didn't necessarily make her a bad person. We all fall out of love. She'd only benefited from coincidence, but at what cost? I wouldn't have wished that even on Patricia.

"Did they catch the men?" I asked, handing her her fifth drink.

"Not yet," she said.

"Wouldn't it look bad for you to leave town?"

"I told them I was visiting my sister in Memphis," she said. "And I told her where I was going, told her that I had to get away for a while. They can find me if they need to."

"I can understand you wanting to get away," I said, "but the new car? The new clothes? New haircut?"

"Everything around me held the death of Arnold," she said. "Even the clothes in my closet, and I couldn't take it."

"It wasn't your fault they shot him. If he hadn't—"

"It was my fault he believed I loved him," she snapped. "He died believing that."

I watched her. She averted her eyes, killed the drink, then fumbled in the pack for another cigarette, hands shaking. Two more cigarettes came out with the one she pinched and they fell onto the coffee table. "I should go," she said, cramming the two cigarettes back into the pack.

"I didn't mean to upset you," I said.

Standing up, she dabbed at her eyes with the bar napkin.

"Are you okay to drive?" I asked. "The road's steep down off this mountain."

"I've driven worse," she said.

I helped her into her coat, and she stepped outside, stopped, then turned around. "I'm okay," she said. "Thanks for the drinks."

From the front porch, I watched her leave, watched her disappear down Parthenon Road, and then listened until the sound of her car was swallowed up by the silent frosty darkness. I stood there a short while longer. The dogs came around the house and sat down at my feet. Still watching the road, I scratched one behind the ears. Then I went back inside, out of the cold.

The next day at the job site, I caught a glimpse of Harris's eyes, red and half-lidded, bags underneath. His face had at least a three-day growth, not that clean-shaven is a requirement for the remodeling industry. Hanging from under his Razorbacks cap, the locks of his peppery-colored hair were greasy and matted. "You look like you've either had a good time or you've been through hell one," I said.

"Baby was up all night, third goddamn night in a row," he said. "The croup."

"Wanna go home and rest?"

"So you can get at that filly?" He managed another grin, but it was clear he was too tired to give me much of a hard time.

"You never know."

"I reckon I can make it till lunch," he said. "We'll have them bathroom fixtures plumbed by then anyways."

"Sounds alright to me," I said. "We can put down the linoleum tomorrow, then get started on the kitchen tiles. I'd like to have it painted and papered by Sunday."

"Alright then," he said. "I'll make up for it this weekend."

As we were unloading linoleum from my truck, two State Police cruisers pulled into the parking lot, the cars clean and glinting in the morning sunlight. The cold front had passed through and a warmer breeze blew from the south. The troopers went to the office. A minute or so later, the owner led them out. For a moment I was afraid she was taking them to Margot's cabin, but she led them to the bow hunters' cabin instead and opened the door.

"Wonder what they want?" Harris asked, staring at them.

"Looks like those guys from Missouri," I said. "Wonder if they have anything to do with the elk?"

"Ain't seen that Bronco of theirs for two days," he said. "Figured they was gone."

I glanced at Margot's cabin, saw her peeking through a narrow part between the curtains in the window. Then she tugged them back together.

Harris and I walked to the bow hunters' cabin. The owner said, "Their families called those two fellers in missing."

Wearing surgical gloves, the troopers carried out a couple of suitcases, plastic bags filled with papers, pencils, bottles of buck lure, arrowheads, pocketknives, beer cans, and convenience store sandwich wrappers. "You fellows been working here all week?" one of the troopers asked us.

"All fall," Harris said.

"When was the last time you saw a green Bronco here?"

"Must've been two days ago," I said. "We figured they'd left for good."

"Anyone else been here this week?"

"In number five," I said. "Don't think she knows any more than we do, though."

"Guess I'll find out," he said and headed in Margot's direction. He knocked a couple of times before she answered. They talked for a few minutes. She shook her head, shrugged her shoulders, and he headed back toward the other troopers.

After hesitating, I went to her cabin, knocked on the door. It cracked open, the chain still fastened and stretched tight.

"Morning," I said.

"Morning." She watched me for a couple of seconds.

"You keep that door chained shut," I said, "and my partner's gonna give me hell all day for striking out."

She unfastened the chain and I stepped inside.

"Look if I upset—"

"It's okay," she said. "I had a nice time—overall."

"I'm glad," I said.

She smiled, then nodded toward the bow hunter's cabin. "What do you think's happened?" she asked.

"Those hunters are probably out partying somewhere," I said, looking around. She'd done a little decorating, and I was glad to see a hint of permanence. Flames in a couple of lead-glass candleholders flickered on the dining table. The air smelled like vanilla. I picked up pictures of an older woman and a teenage boy from the counter near the TV and examined the faces for traces of Margot.

"That's my mom and my brother," she said. "The only bad part about disappearing is missing them."

"They don't know where you are?"

"They know," she said. "But that doesn't make them any closer."

I glanced at the pictures again. "Your brother looks a lot younger than you," I said.

"He came along late. An accident," she said. "We're close. I practically raised him because Mother always worked." She looked at me, smiled a little.

"Are you here just to trace my family's roots?"

"Well, no," I said. "How'd you like to see something beautiful this evening?"

"Do we have to talk about the past?"

"Nope, we don't have to."

"Well," she said. "How can a girl turn something beautiful down?"

"Three o'clock?"

"You know where to find me."

Outside, the troopers taped the hunters' cabin off with yellow police tape. As I approached number four, Harris was waiting on me.

"Got a date?" he asked, grinning again.

"Yep," I said. "Think I'll take her down to Steele's Creek, show her the elk while there are still some left."

"That orta make her swoon," he said, rolling his bloodshot eyes.

"Of course elk-watching requires a bottle or two of wine and a picnic basket."

"Wine? Picnic baskets?" he said. "Jesus."

"Women like that shit," I said.

"Till you marry them," he said. "Then they like money and babies. I know, I been through three now, and all they wanted was money and babies. Same old shit, man."

"Mine seemed to want money more than babies, but she took them too," I said. "And hell, she made twice as much as I did. We had separate checking accounts. Her idea."

"Wouldn't of been if you'd made more."

"Probably not."

He smiled. "She taught you some refinement, though, huh?"

"Yep," I said. "Because of her, I know which side of the plate to put my salad fork on."

"Shit." He shook his head again, went inside. The cops poked around in the cabin for a couple of more hours, then took off.

"It's beautiful," Margot said, gazing up at the gray cliffs across the narrow river. The valley was wide here, at Steele's Creek, where the tiny stream dumped into the Buffalo. Here were campgrounds, horse barns, a canoe launch. The caretaker, a retired man from Michigan, lived in an old ranch-style stone house, taken over by the government after the land was bought.

We were parked at the canoe launch. This was the time of year when the dry season gives way to the wet. The water was low and clear, but that would change soon, and the river would become swift and green and scour away the skin of leaves that lined the stream bottom in the slack water.

"God sure knew what He was doing when He created this," she said.

"See those lines etched in the limestone wall?" I said, pointing at the cliffs. The rock face is mostly smooth, except for the horizontal lines every few feet. You can mark significant changes in the water level over the centuries much like you can count the rings of a tree to figure its age. As an engineer, I learned just enough about the physics of nature to not believe in creation.

"Yes," she said.

"The river's done that over time, always eroding this canyon," I said. "Would it be fair to give God all the credit for the river's work?"

"Well," she said. "God's the one who put it all in motion. Like Adam and Eve, a river's been given free reign to make its own way." She gazed downstream, where the river bent against another high rock face on our side and disappeared behind a sandstone gravel bar.

"Is that what you're doing now?" I asked. "Making your own way?"

"I suppose it is," she said. "And it's about as hard as wearing down that rock." She scanned the fields behind me, then glanced at me. "Now where are those elk you've talked so much about?"

We drove out of Steele Creek and headed toward Ponca, crossed the bridge over the river and parked beneath it. Fields lay to the south of the road, and nine elk, scattered about, grazed in the closest. Standing near the tree line along the back of the field, near the river, a large bull whistled.

"Wow," Margot said. "I've heard that on TV, but it's a strange sound in person."

"The females seem to like it."

"Give me flowers any day," she said.

"How about wine instead?"

We eased into the edge of the field, spread out a blanket, unpacked the basket, uncorked the wine, and filled two glasses. "To the mountains," I said, and we toasted.

After she sipped the wine, she watched a couple of young bulls sparring near an uninterested cow. The clacking of their interlocked antlers echoed along the river. A car passed on the bridge, slowing so the driver could look at the elk. A few people had gathered at the split-rail fence a little farther down the road to watch and take photos. She gazed at the ridges around us. "Reminds me so much of home," she said.

"Tennessee?"

She nodded. "Definitely not Fort Worth."

"I've driven through east Tennessee a couple of times," I said. "Pretty country."

"Yes it is," she said. "Like this, only the mountains are bigger there."

"But no elk."

"Nope. No elk."

As we ate the pastrami, provolone, Roma tomatoes, red leaf lettuce, and stone-ground mustard on pumpernickel, I watched her slow, careful observations of the river valley. She took it in a little at a time, as if committing it to memory. The dread that she might not be long for the area rose in me. "What's it like to have someone killed right next to you?" I asked.

She looked at me, as if taken off guard a little. "I thought the past was off limits."

"Well, to tell you the truth, I can't stop wondering about it."

"Neither can I." She downed the glass of wine and averted her eyes.

"You don't have to talk," I said.

"Well," she said. "After last night it doesn't seem so bad."

"Your husband's death?"

"No," she said. "Talking about it." She poured more wine.

"It's nothing like you expect. I mean, not like what you've always seen on TV or in the movies. In real life, it's fast and loud." She held the uncorked bottle in one hand, sipped from the glass in the other. "And there's this silence that follows right after the gunshot, like the volume of the whole world has been turned down. There's this emptiness."

In a way I knew what she meant.

"I felt terror, at first," she said. "I thought I was dead for sure. Then, when they left, I saw the blood and felt sick. I threw up. I cried until I drained myself."

"Because he was shot?"

Corking the bottle, she said, "Because I wasn't." She drank again, then looked off at the elk.

"I thought you begged them not to."

"When your life's on the line, the only thing that you think about is living. When you have time to think about it later, that's when you start changing your mind."

"Well, I'm glad self-preservation kicked in," I said.

She glanced at me and smiled, then looked away again. We were silent for a while, listening to the bull elk whistle. Crows cawed from the woods across the river. A speck of a plane threaded two thin jet trails across the sky. Finally, she looked at me. "What's the goriest thing you've ever seen?"

"Outside of the sewage treatment plant?"

"Yes," she said. "Ever seen a dead person, except for in a funeral home?"

"Just my grandmother," I said. "I was with my dad when he found her. She never woke up from her sleep. But, to me, she looked like she was still sleeping."

"You've had it easy then," she said, returning her gaze to the elk.

Glancing at the sky, I nodded. The jet was gone, its trail growing ragged. We didn't talk much more the rest of the afternoon, and I felt my connection to her fading like those contrails overhead.

Back at my house, I built a fire in the stove. This time, Margot and I sat on the couch together. There was still some Maker's Mark left over from her last visit. I mixed a couple of drinks.

Wanting to create something between us for us to latch onto, I looked at her and said, "You know, Margot, meeting you almost makes me wanna believe in fate."

She smiled and said, "I believe I'd like you to sit a little closer."

I slid next to her, set my drink on the coffee table. I started to say more, but she said, "Shhh," and placed two fingers against my lips. I took her arm by the wrist and lowered her hand. I leaned my face into hers and we kissed. A short one at first, then longer. That rose fragrance. With my arm around her, holding her tightly to me, she felt like something that should always be there. Her hand came to a rest on my check. After we kissed, I stood and took her hand to help her from the couch. She hesitated, but I gripped a little more firmly and looked her in the eyes. For once, she didn't glance away. She stood and I led her into my bedroom.

The next morning, I dressed for work, leaving her lying in bed, a crazy quilt draped over her. She was the first woman to still be in my bed the next morning since Patricia. I kissed Margot's forehead, watched her stir a little, and wanted to stay there with her. But I knew I had to work, had to face Harris, and he'd tell by the look in my eye what had happened. A whole day of ribbing was in store for me, but I didn't mind. I left her a note on the dresser saying I'd be back at lunch.

Harris was already working in number four, cementing tile to the bathroom walls, when I got there. He glanced at me, then concentrated on his work. "Have a good time?"

"Yeah," I said. "But excuse me if I don't reveal the details."

"Every man's got a private side," he said. "And it ought to stay that way."

Digging for a trowel in the toolbox, I watched him from the corner of my eye. "A damn good philosophy."

A little after noon, Margot's car was gone when I pulled into the driveway. I went inside, looked for a note. I found mine, on the kitchen counter, with no reply. The bed hadn't been made, but she'd showered. An extra towel was wet. She hadn't returned to her cabin, at least not while I was there.

Ten minutes later, back at the tourist court, Harris was still at lunch. I asked the owner if she'd checked out.

"Not long after you left," the old woman said.

"See which way she went?"

"Turned left out of here."

Which meant she either went up Route 74 past my place or up Route 7 toward Harrison. If she were trying to elude me, she wouldn't take 74. Took 7 toward Harrison, knowing she had a good fifteen minutes on me. Hopefully the twisting road would slow her enough to allow me to catch up. Once she got to Harrison, there were any number of directions she could go. And she'd left no hint about where she might go next, except maybe East Tennessee.

Two miles out of Jasper, I overtook a Tyson's truck, hauling chickens, going every bit of twenty-five. Feathers snowed down on me, and in the rearview, chicken feather devils twisted in the wake of my truck. Veering in and out of the left lane whenever the striped lines marked a passing zone, I followed him for five miles before I could pass, cussing out loud. Within another mile, I was behind a kindergarten bus, stopping every fifty or so yards, it seemed, the stop sign flapping out from the side of the bus like a busted wing.

The trip to Harrison took forty-five minutes. From there, I traveled 65 north to the Missouri line, but saw no sign of her. I pulled over to the side of the road and sat there a few minutes, watching the road as if her car might appear over the rise. The good feeling that had begun to replenish me over the last several days slowly leached out and drained away. I watched the road for a while longer before turning around, then coasting past the KKK's roadside clean-up sign on my way back to Jasper.

After work, I drove home, hoping her car would be there, but the driveway was empty, except for the dogs stretched out across the asphalt, catching the last of the sun.

Inside, my answering machine was silent, no beep and flashing red light holding the promise of her voice. I went to the bathroom, lifted the towel from the bar. It had mostly dried, except for dampness where it had been folded over the bar. I held it to my cheek, the last remnant of her presence cool and drying in the terry of the towel.

For a while I sipped the rest of the Maker's Mark, my fingers rotating the glass. The phone rang. I was so focused on Margot's absence, I barely heard the first ring. Then my brain kicked in. I slammed the glass on the end table, scrambled from the couch, grabbed the receiver just after the second ring and said hello.

"Frank?" she said.

"Where are you?" I asked.

"Frank, I was going to call you to just thank you for being so kind," she said. "But I can't stop thinking about you. I . . . I can't think about what to do next without being distracted by you."

"Where are you?"

"Springfield," she said. "It was as far as I could get. I've been sitting in a restaurant for three hours trying not to call you."

"Come back," I said. "Please. Come back."

There was a pause. I could hear dishes clanking, people talking.

"Frank, I can't give enough back," she almost whispered. "I'm just not ready."

"I'll take whatever you have," I said.

"Frank," she said. Another pause. Christmas music played in the background.

"What is it, Margot? What?"

"Frank, I'm on my way." She hung up.

The next two hours were excruciating. Every so often I'd want to take off for Springfield, in case she was lying. But why would she lie? And if she were, what good would it do for me to go after her? Lying would prove she didn't want to come back. But then why would she call?

Pacing, I listened for the dogs to announce her arrival, for the drone of her motor, for the whine of her tires on the road. Then I stood at the window and watched for her. Occasionally, a pair of headlights came down Parthenon Road, and I rushed to the front door, flung it open, waiting for Margot to pull into the drive. After the car passed, I closed the door back and paced again.

Finally, her lights swung from the road into my living room window, the dogs barking. I opened the front door, sent them to the back yard. She climbed from her Saturn and crept toward me. I was hoping for a mad dash, a collision of embraces, but I waited and watched. She stopped at the bottom of the three steps to the front porch. "I'm tired of running, Frank," she said, nearly crying.

"Come in," I said. "Come on in to my house."

That Saturday night, Milton and I rode along the top of the bluffs instead of along the river. These trails were for hikers only, but we decided to alter our course to get a better perspective. We were approaching the Boy Scout camp when he said, "They found them two hunters today."

"They okay?"

"Dead. Both of them," he said. "Found them down near Hasty, but they'd been moved there from somewheres else."

"Something to do with the meth labs?" I asked.

"Looks like it. Them hunters stumbled up on one probably."

"Jesus."

He stopped Cahill. I pulled up alongside him. "They don't want us doing the patrols no more," he said.

"Who?"

"Them rangers."

"Now's a good time to tell me," I said.

"They think it's too risky for us."

"Well, they might be right."

"Hell, I don't care about no meth labs," he said. "I'm worried about the elk. Now them rangers are gonna be so focused on finding labs the elk are gonna be even more vulnerable."

"Might be true," I said. "But I don't mind admitting I'd rather be home right now."

He spurred Cahill back into motion. "Got that lady staying with you now?"

Riding behind him, I looked at his back bobbing in the saddle in the quarter moon light. "How'd you know?"

"Small town, Frank," he said. "They said she moved out of the cabin on Thursday."

"Wasn't like she had much to move."

"What's she hiding from? A jealous husband?"

"Don't know," I said, not wanting to tell her story. "But I'm glad she's hiding with me."

"You a lucky man," he said. "Have a woman just show up like that out here in the middle of nowhere. Ever wonder why?"

"Well, yeah," I said. "But you've heard that old saying about gift horses."

"There's also one about too good to be true."

I stopped my horse and watched him for a few moments before following again.

Another mile or so up the trail, Milton halted his horse again and said, "Listen."

I stopped, steadied Jack Cutter. Around the bend, a motorcycle droned down the trail along the river, came around a curve, then crossed the river to the other side. We watched its light probe the woods, jerking from the rough trail. Where the canyon widened, the bike veered into a field overgrown with cedars, its taillight disappearing and reappearing. It climbed the gorge on the other side. A few seconds later, there was a flash, like a polaroid being taken, then the sound of a muffled explosion, like a shotgun blast into a pillow.

Our horses recoiled. "Easy, Cahill," Milton said, then reached for Jack Cutter's bridle to calm him too.

We listened for several more moments. The bike was still idling.

Milton started off. I let him go a few yards, thinking about those two hunters from Missouri. "Milton," I said, "Maybe we should just go to the rangers."

"Come on," he said, turning Cahill toward me. "If it's a meth lab, they gonna get out quick as they can."

"Then who's the guy on the bike?"

"Liable to be our elk killer." He turned, kicked Cahill into a trot. We eased down the steep slope to the river, where it bent, where the motorcycle had forded it. Crossing the shallow water, lulled into the rhythm of the horse, I watched the moonlit edges of the ripples and eddies. A blast came from upstream, from a still, deep pool twenty or thirty yards away. Jack Cutter reared up on his hind legs and whinnied. I looked down. The cold water swirled around the legs of the horse. He dropped back to all fours and was ready to buck. Milton turned Cahill around and grabbed Jack Cutter by the bridle again and yanked the horse's head to his chest. Cahill stood firm in the water. Milton leaned into the horse's ear and said, "Whoa, Jack Cutter." The horse flinched a little but seemed to be calming down. Its breathing began to steady. "It's all right," Milton said to him. He released Jack Cutter's head and grabbed the reins where they were attached to the bridle and led us across the river.

"What was that?"

"A beaver," he said. "Smacking his tail on the water."

We hit the trail at a trot, knowing the path was clear of low-hanging tree limbs. We estimated where the motorcycle had turned into the field and listened for the idling bike. It had stalled out, but a voice was yelling for help. We followed it.

The man had dragged himself along a large, moss-covered log. He looked at us, eyes wild in Milton's flashlight beam. We dismounted, tied the horses off, and started toward him. He wore camouflaged coveralls, the front torn and slick with blood. He looked to be a little older than I was. "Don't kill me," he said, struggling to get the words out.

"It's all right," Milton said. "We're gonna get you out of here."

I shone my light on his motorcycle and walked toward it. The front wheel and handlebars had been blown away. The rest lay there like some headless animal. Lying next to the bike was a crossbow. "He's got a crossbow," I said.

"You been killing the elk, ain't you?" Milton said to the man.

"Fucking guv'ment," the man gasped.

"Goddamn elk killer," Milton said. Then he turned toward me.

"Don't step nowheres you ain't already stepped, Frank."

"What?"

"Landmines."

"Fuck," I said and looked at the ground around me. I couldn't make out any unusual humps in the dirt, any signs of mines. "Hell, Milton, I don't know where I stepped."

"You better remember," Milton said. "Now ease back to the horses and get me that First Aid kit out of my saddlebags. We're gonna need to patch him up a little."

"I'm afraid to move, Milton."

"Dammit, we can't just stand in place all night," he said. "See if you can find your footprints."

"Jesus, Milton." I shone my light on the ground to locate my footprints. Some were visible in the loose dirt and moldering leaves. The others I had to calculate. I took a deep breath and walked on those prints as if they were stones leading across the river and made it back to the horses. As I was digging through Milton's bag for the kit, I heard the zipper of the coveralls come down. Then Milton said, "Oh, Jesus." He lurched up, staggered off to the side.

"Milton," I called out. "The land mines."

He stopped. His arms flew out as if he were trying to balance himself, and he leaned against a tree, head lolled forward. His shoulders rose and fell with his heavy breathing.

"Never mind the First Aid kit," he said.

I snapped the bag shut, then crept toward the man, my light on him. Glistening intestines hung from a gash in his gut. He held his hand over them as if to stuff them back in. Under the blood on his hand was a wedding ring. "I can't feel my legs," he said. He was sobbing now, face slick with muddy sweat. He rolled his eyes up at me, their whites exaggerated.

"What're we gonna do, Milton?" I said.

"He'll never make it out of here. You radio the rangers. We'll have to keep the possums and coyotes away from him."

I clicked off my light, and the man dissolved into the darkness along the ground. I tiptoed back to Milton's horse. Before I could grab the walkie-talkie from his saddlebag, the woods began wheeling in the periphery of my vision. I tried to blink them inert. Bile rose in the back of my throat. For a few moments, I stood in the darkness and listened to the river and the silence that cloaked the canyon. A mist was rising from the water and, straight above me, in the mouth of the gorge, I could see a narrow strip of sky—all that was available to see. I felt closed in and alone and I wanted nothing more than to be with Margot, than to have been with her all night, than to not have my own dead-body story now to tell her. The bile reached my tongue, and I staggered away from the horse and vomited.

It was after daylight when I got home. Margot was up, sitting at the kitchen table, sipping coffee. The sections of the Sunday *Democrat Gazette* were scattered before her. "I barely slept," she said.

"Sorry," I said. "Long night." I told her about the guy on the motorcycle, the land mine. "He was dead by the time the rangers got there," I said. "They carted him out with a four-wheeler and a trailer. Milton's pretty shook up about it."

"What about you?"

I poured a cup of coffee, sat down across from her. "Well, I've seen a dead man now," I said, then took a sip and swallowed hard.

We sat there a while, not talking. I glanced at the newspaper. The left column on the front page was reserved for anecdotes about bizarre crimes, inept criminals and the like. There was a brief story about a man being caught in Asheville, North Carolina, after bragging in a bar to an off-duty cop about his connection with a murder/robbery in Triple Oaks, West Virginia. A couple returning home from a party was robbed as they entered their house. The husband was shot, the wife escaped. Her name was Helen Spangler.

"You see this?" I asked Margot.

"What?" she said.

I slid the paper to her, pointed at the story. "Sounds kind of like your story."

"I saw it," she said, staring off through the kitchen window. She squeezed a napkin in her fist.

I watched her a moment longer, then poured myself the last cup of coffee and made a new pot. In the living room, I stoked the stove, and we sat on the couch, Margot leaning into me, her legs folded under her on the cushions. I put my arm around her, pulled her even closer, and we stared at the stove, at the orange flickers in the vent holes at the bottom of the door. The wind picked up outside, and the stove sucked air, drawing more flame from the logs. Occasionally the fire crackled and orange sparks shot from the vent, scattering across the clay tile hearth before fading to gray and black.

That evening, Milton dropped by. I hung up his coat, and we headed into the living room where I introduced him to Margot.

"Good meeting you finally," he said.

"Sorry about last night," she said as I made drinks.

"Nothing that could of been done," he said, sitting in the straight-back rocker. "Except put a stop to the meanness." He took a sip of bourbon, stared at the stove. Heat waves from the cast iron muddled the wall behind it. "Jesus," he said. "This close to Christmas."

"Who was he?" I asked.

"Cody Hedge," he said. "From Low Gap. His family owned a bunch of that land down around Steele's Creek. He went to Vietnam, then served another term, came back, found out his family's farm went from eight-hundred some-odd acres to barely sixty. They got a fair price, like everybody, but you can't put a price on a family's legacy."

"Took him long enough to act," I said.

"He waited till his old man died," he said. "Least that's what I figured. Charlie Hedge died not long before we started finding the elk dead."

"Why?" Margot asked.

"Hell, who knows? The old man probably felt enough shame from losing the land. Cody might of thought he'd cause him even more if he ever got caught. I don't reckon he figured on no meth labs and boobytraps."

We sat quietly for a few minutes. I poured another round.

"What I wanna know is," Milton said, "what kind of man kills indiscriminate like that?"

"A desperate one," Margot said. "An evil one would take time to plan it out."

"Probably right," he said.

We finished that round. I offered to make another, but Milton said no. He stood, put on his coat. Then he looked at me. "If you wanna stop going on the patrols with me, I don't blame you none."

"Didn't we find the elk killer?" I asked.

"Rangers found a dozen more boobytraps today. And in the old out-building, there wasn't no meth equipment. There had been, but it had been moved. They left the mines, though, and a few hundred pounds of waste. They're fucking up that river, and they killed the boy of a good man. I can't let that pass. There are worse enemies now than elk killers."

"And more dangerous," Margot said.

"Dangerous or not," he said, "I plan on finding the bastards. They done brought their shit to the wrong part of the world." He looked at me. "You still in?"

I glanced at Margot again. She was shaking her head and for good reason, but I felt even more responsible for going now. He'd have gone alone, and if something happened to him, I'd never live it down. "I've got to," I said to her.

"Alright then," Milton said. "See you Saturday."

After he left, she said, "This isn't your all's fight anymore, Frank."

"Milton feels like these mountains are his country," I said. "And if I wanna really feel like I'm a part of them too, I need to help out."

"Frank, I just met you," she said. "I could've left too. But I came back. Because of you. So don't do anything that's gonna get you taken away from me. You're a part of me now too."

"And I'm glad." I smiled at her. "We'll just watch from a distance and make calls," I said. "I'll see to that."

Worry would not undo the furrows in her brow or release the frown on her face. I took her by the hand, pulled her to me. I held her, trying to reassure her.

On Monday, the temperature had dipped into the teens, but the sky was clear and blue. The wind was still. I beat Harris to the tourist court by a good half hour, and I was a little late. He'd let his three-day growth become a beard, which was streaked with white, adding ten or fifteen years to his age. He had on tree bark camouflage, knees and chest stained from dirt and oil.

"Get a job in a truck stop?" I asked.

"I wish," he said. "My brother-in-law's got an old diesel GMC he's trying to get running. I was helping him yesterday."

"Worst engines on the road."

"Hell, all they did was bore out a regular engine," he said. "You gotta start new. You can't just modify what you already got, like they did."

We were starting on number five today, Margot's cabin. First thing was to tear the ceiling tiles out. We put on our safety goggles and hard hats, carried crowbars, long-handled pry bars, and claw hammers inside.

"You know Cody Hedges?" I asked.

"Heard about that," he said. "A damn shame."

"I saw it happen."

"You and Milton?"

"Yeah."

"Newspaper didn't mention your names."

"'Two civilian patrolmen,'" I said. "That's me and Milton. They didn't want to give out our identities, afraid someone might take offense at us."

"Y'all better be careful down there," he said.

"You and Cody in Vietnam at the same time?"

"Yeah," he said. "Two different places though. He was a Marine. Survived Khe Sahn, then got it here. Damn."

"I'm thinking about trying to talk Milton out of going on any more patrols."

"I would if I was you," he said, reaching his pry bar toward the ceiling. He wedged the forked end into the seam between the panels and pushed it through the tile. "He got who he was after. Now he ought to leave well enough alone."

"I agree," I said. "Don't think he will, though."

He stopped probing, the pry bar still stabbing the ceiling. "Well, dammit, for his sake and yours, you better talk him out of it. You get killed down there, who am I gonna work for? I damn sure don't wanna go back and work in no chicken plant." He shoved on the bar, ripping the composite material of the ceiling tile. Flecks of brown cardboard-like particles snowed down. Probing beneath the tile, he found a nail and wrestled it from the ceiling joist. The tiles sagged. He found another nail, yanked it out, and several tiles fell to the floor. The rest came down within a half hour.

That Friday, after work, I stopped by Milton's house to try to talk him out of the patrol. The white turkey gobbled at my arrival, stirring up his hounds. They all came to me, the turkey included, sniffing my dogs on my legs.

Inside, Milton was watching *Jeopardy*. Under his Christmas tree were presents for his sons' families. He told me to get a beer out of the fridge.

"The rangers have found seven houses total that have been used for meth labs," he said.

I opened a beer. "Seven?"

"All of them mined. Those old gobs of waste left behind. What if some kids wandered in there?"

"Well, we know the answer to that."

"I think I got a line on where the next one might be," he said.

"Oh yeah?"

He unrolled a USGS map on the kitchen table. The upper third of the river snaked across the page. Contours showed the steepness of the bluffs, the gradual slope of the valley floor opposite them.

Highlighted were the seven buildings where the labs had been found. Other buildings were shown, some near the water and others up on the mountainsides, but they had not been marked. There appeared to be no particular pattern to their being used, except that none of the buildings were particularly close to the trails or river. He pointed to an old house in a U in the river. "That's where the rangers think they'll be," he said.

"Looks like as good a guess as a man could make to me."

"Well, it's the wrong guess." He pointed to a dashed dead-end road that branched from another dashed road that stretched from Route 74 to Route 7, about fifteen miles. Using a drafting compass, he placed a leg on the end of the road and set the other leg on the farthest barn in which a lab had been found. He drew a circle with its center at the end of the road. The river snaked in and out of the perimeter of the circle. All the marked buildings and one unmarked one fell within the circle. The suspected house didn't.

I looked at him. "Why didn't you tell the rangers?"

"I just figured out a little while ago," he said. "I'd almost forgot about that old road."

"Bullshit, Milton."

"Oh, hell," he said. "Don't you wanna make a statement to those assholes?"

"Statement?"

"I want, by God, to show people they can't just come in here and blow the sons of good men to kingdom come."

"Milton," I said. "The man was killing the elk."

"And I can understand why," he said. "But I can't understand these evil sonsabitches."

"Let's let the law—"

"The hell with the law," he said, staring at me, his eyes and breath testifying to an entire afternoon of beer drinking. "They the ones that got that Hedges boy killed. If they had left people in them houses, wouldn't be no meth labs in them now."

"Milton, that's not very logical."

"Logic? You college boys and your damn logic." He finished off his can of beer. "I'll go by my goddamn self if I got to."

Looking at him, I saw the face of man who would defend his homeland and the people in it, no matter what. Everyone was leaving, and only strangers like me or troublemakers like the meth cookers were taking their place. Before I could respond, he rose, went to the tree. He pulled out a package—a video tape, I could tell—and handed it to me. "Merry Christmas," he said.

"Hell, Milton—"

"It ain't nothing," he said. "Open it."

"It's three weeks till Christmas."

"Hell, Christmas ain't a day, it's spiritual. Open it."

I did and the movie was *Big Jake.*

"Study on that movie," Milton said. "It shows you can't just run roughshod over somebody's land."

"Thanks, Milton," I said. "But I haven't—"

"Don't worry about it," he said. "As long as you help me out, that's all the present I need."

"Well," I said. "Count me in." I downed my beer, stood.

"You a good man, Frank," he said. "At first I thought you was a little soft. But you a good man. I feel like I can trust you."

"I'll do my best," I said.

"I know you will."

At home, Margot was in the bath. Her purse was on the dresser in my bedroom. Thinking of that murder in West Virginia, I stared at the purse for nearly a minute, then unzipped it, pulled out her wallet. There was no driver's license, no identification, no credit cards, no checks—only cash. Hands shaking, I folded the purse back together, then snapped it shut. I released the breath I didn't realize I'd been holding, put the wallet back in her purse. I sighed, then poured two bourbon and sodas and carried them to the bathroom. In the clawfoot tub, she was up to her chin in bubble bath. I handed her one of the drinks and we toasted.

"What should we drink to?" she said.

"To you coming back."

We clinked the glasses together, knocked back the drinks. She looked at me. "Frank, don't go with Milton," she said. "I don't know what I'd do if you didn't come back." She reached for my hand, the warm moistness and softness of hers startling against the calluses, scars, and scabs on mine. "Do you believe me?"

I stared into her eyes, wide with earnestness, and wanted to see the truth. Her face was expectant, waiting, but unrevealing. I pulled my hand away. "Why don't you have a driver's license?"

"You looked in—"

"Where's your driver's license, Margot?" I asked. "And is that even your name?"

Her trembling hands gripped the lip of the tub. "Yes, Frank, it's my name," she said. "I told you I was trying to escape everything."

"How can I be sure?"

"That's why I'm here, Frank."

"In Jasper?"

She watched me for a moment, then took my hand again. "With you." She smiled. "Help me out."

I took her hand and helped her from the tub. I dried her off with a long towel, gliding it along the curves of her body, over her ribs and stomach, over her breasts and hardening nipples, over the swell of her hips. I felt as if I were sculpting her, as if I were making her into someone new, someone without a mysterious past. I dropped the towel to the floor and we kissed and she undid my shirt and jeans.

In bed she was on top of me, moving against me, her palms against my chest, nails digging into me. The silhouette of her body was the color of a storm in the darkness of the room. For several minutes I ran my hands along her ribs, my finger tips along the recesses between each one. Then I held her at the taper of her waist and closed my eyes and found her rhythm and pulled her to me and felt her wash over me and draw me in deeper.

Saturday night, on the trail along the river, Milton and I headed for that house. The air was cold and still and heavy. A few inches of snow had been predicted.

Margot wasn't happy that I'd come out here. Before I left, she kissed me, her face forced into mine. She held me tighter and longer than I'd expected. As she turned away, I could see her eyes moistening. But she was the real reason I'd decided to go along with Milton: I wanted to test her, to find out how important I really was to her.

From the top of a small ridge, a hundred yards or so away, Milton and I observed the house with binoculars. We were hidden in the trees. Hoping Milton would be wrong about the house, I saw its broken out windows were dim rectangles of orange, and I clenched my teeth and closed my eyes for several seconds. I opened my eyes, trying to blink away the dread. In the house, light smoke rolled from the tops of the windows then flattened in the sky—confirming the coming snow. We could see the shadows of a couple of men moving inside. Two dirt bikes and a four-wheeler were parked outside.

I looked at Milton, the features of his face barely distinguishable under the brim of his hat and in the backdrop of forest. The river gurgled in the gorge behind him.

"Well," he said. "Let's tie the horses up here, go get a closer look."

"Let's just radio the rangers, Milton."

"I got something to settle with them bastards," he said, climbing down from Cahill and tying him off. He pulled his shotgun from its scabbard and started toward the old house.

"Dammit, Milton," I said. I dismounted, tied Jack Cutter off, grabbed my twenty-gauge pump. "Wait up," I whispered as loudly as I could without being heard.

The house was in a flat now covered by a stand of thin locusts and egg-shaped cedars that had started growing after the people moved out. Twenty years ago, the property had likely been planted with corn, pole beans, and tomatoes.

We stopped at the edge of the flat. "Better circle around," Milton whispered. "Might be boobytraps all over. We'll head for the house the same way they come in," he whispered. "They ain't gonna mine their own trail."

We stayed in the dense woods, circling the house until we found a trail rutted through the leaves and mud. Then we left the forest, entering the flat on a belly crawl. About fifty yards away, we paused. We were downwind now. A bitter smell hung in the air. "Smell that?" he whispered.

"That's all we need to know," I said and looked at him, not wanting to go any nearer to that house. "Let's crawl back out of here and call the rangers."

He looked through the binoculars, then lowered them. "I'm going in," he said.

I grabbed his arm. "No, Milton," I said. "Those guys mean business."

He glared at me. "So do I." He yanked his arm away.

"You saw what happened to those bow hunters."

"They didn't know what they was getting into."

"Do you?"

He looked at the house again. "Yep," he said. "But them bastards don't know what's coming."

"Dammit, Milton," I said. "This ain't a John Wayne movie."

He scowled at me again. "This is our big chance, Frank."

"Milton, those guys would as soon kill you as look at you. They don't care. You do. And if they kill you, this place doesn't have a soul to watch over it."

"Everybody's gotta die sooner or later."

"What about those grandkids of yours?" I said. "All those

presents you bought them won't take your place."

His face softened.

"And, besides," I said, "I'm too citified to take over for you."

He looked at the house for a few seconds, then at me.

"Let's let the authorities handle it."

"Alright then," he said. "Maybe you're right."

I lolled my head toward the ground, felt the tension release in my back.

We crawled backwards until we made the woods, then crouched and eased back toward the horses. We hadn't gone far when a bright flash of light and a blast came from directly in front of us. Milton staggered back. I saw a figure in the darkness. My right arm stung, but I shot at the figure and dove on the ground. The figure fired again, but this time into the fallen leaves. The figure staggered, then fell. For several moments silence took over.

"What's going on?" someone yelled from the house.

"Milton?" I whispered.

"Goddamn," he cried. "Goddamn. Chest."

"Let's get the hell outta here," another voice said from the house. A motorcycle started up. "Where you going, man?" the first voice called out.

I could see a figure coming toward us from the house.

The guy on the bike headed up the mountain toward the dead-end road.

"Justin?" the figure said, still coming. "I told you not to shoot at nobody else. Justin?"

The voice started registering, but my right arm stung, drawing my attention away from the man. I felt above the elbow. My coat was moist with blood. I'd caught spray from the shotgun. I climbed to one knee, aimed my flashlight and gun in the direction of the approaching figure.

"Frank, is that you?" he said, and I knew who it was. I closed my eyes for a moment and grimaced, trying not to scream out at him. "Milton?" he called out.

"Milton's hurt bad, Harris," I said.

"Dammit, Frank," Harris said. "Goddammit." He kicked around in the leaves. Nearly sobbing, he said, "You said you were talking him out of this."

Milton coughed, moaned, worked his legs in the leaves.

"Milton's in trouble, Harris. We gotta get him out of here."

"I can't do it," he said. "You know I can't."

"I'm turning you in, regardless," I said. "Might as well make it look better by helping Milton."

"Take the four-wheeler," he said. He looked in the other figure's direction. "He ain't gonna need it no more. I told him not to be taking the shit."

"Harris, you gotta come with me."

"Frank, watch out!" Harris yelled, pointing at the other figure. I saw him from the corner of my eye, struggling to his knees, trying to level his gun at me. I wheeled, pumped, fired. My shotgun kicked. The man's body toppled to the ground.

"God," Milton groaned, then gasped and coughed.

I aimed at Harris now. "Don't move, Harris. Don't make me shoot you too."

"I ain't got no gun on me," he said. "And Frank, I ain't shot nobody. Now I'm gonna get on out of here." He turned back to the house, started walking again.

"Harris," I said, holding the bead on the shotgun barrel on the silhouette of his back. He stopped.

"Here's your chance, Frank."

I put a little pressure on the trigger, closed my left eye, took a breath. Milton coughed again but barely moved. I pulled my finger from the trigger guard, closed both eyes, hung my head, and lowered the gun. I heard him run. He kick-started the bike, took off up the mountain.

I went to the other man, shone the light on him. He lay on his right side. His left shoulder was mangled from my first shot, his left side from my second. A few holes from stray shot freckled his neck and jaw. He wasn't more than eighteen or nineteen. His mouth was agape. His eyes looked silver. Festering acne covered his face. He was emaciated, like a man being starved. I nudged him with the toe of my boot. He didn't move. I rolled him onto his back. On a thin chain around his neck was a locket. I started to open it, but I didn't want to see some girlfriend or wife or kid.

I grabbed my gun by the barrel and slung it into the woods and hauled Milton out on the four-wheeler, stopping at the rangers' station, where we waited on the state troopers and the ambulances. The rangers questioned us, but Milton was barely hanging on. He managed to tell them they'd shot first. Soon after, he died. I'd called Margot too, told her meet me at the hospital in Harrison, where they'd take Milton and me after I'd answered their questions.

"You recognize them?" a trooper asked me at the hospital.

I looked at him, his face nondescript, chin sharp, eyes hard and green, a flat-top haircut. I remembered the tired look in Harris's eyes the last couple of weeks. I thought of his wife and kid, his screaming that warning. "It was dark," I said. "Could've been anyone."

"There were two? You're sure of that?"

I nodded. He watched me a while longer, then told me I could go.

When I walked out of the emergency room, Margot was sitting in the waiting room. They'd removed seven pieces of lead shot from my arm and wrapped it with gauze. She came to me, took my good arm and led me to her car.

Driving home, she kept glancing at me, but she didn't pry. I stayed quiet.

At the house, she helped me undress and set me on the edge of the bed. She ran her fingers across the gauze that choked my arm. It was still numb and I couldn't feel her touch there.

"Harris was one of them," I said.

"The guy who works for you?"

"He saved my life," I said. "Then I let him go." I felt myself breaking down, something I couldn't control slamming against my insides and my brain. "I was mad enough, I hated him enough, but I couldn't shoot him. Once I saw I was safe, I couldn't shoot anymore."

She ran her fingers through my hair. "It's alright," she said. "I know what you've been through."

"Do you?" I asked. "I mean, my own employee turns out to be a meth cooker. My friend gets shot. I shot a man. You show up here from out of nowhere without a driver's license. I don't know who to trust. Do you really know what I've been through?"

She leaned her head against my shoulder and looked at our reflections in the dresser mirror. "Yes," she said. "I know what it's like to watch someone be killed." She stopped, blinked away tears. "To feel guilty about being alive."

I turned toward her, grabbed her arm, and said, "Are you telling me the truth?" She looked at me. "Are you?"

"Every day," she said, "I wonder why I deserve to be alive. Every day. Every goddamn day."

I released her arm, and she stood. She took a tissue from the decorative box she'd bought and placed on the dresser, and she dabbed her eyes. She grabbed her robe and headed into the bathroom. I sat there, looking at myself in the mirror with only my reflection looking back.

On Tuesday, I was a pallbearer for Milton, along with his three sons, who came in from Dallas, Tulsa, and Kansas City, and his two surviving brothers who lived in Harrison. All of them told me Milton's death wasn't my fault, but their words seemed to hold up no better than a two-by-four could hold up a bridge. I sweated through the entire service, staring at the poinsettias surrounding the casket.

Afterward, I told Margot that I had to get away for a little while, that I was sure she could relate.

"But I want you to be here when I get back," I said.

She looked at the ground for a moment, then said, "I love you, Frank. Remember that." She kissed me, opened the truck door for me. I climbed in, looked at her and wondered why I couldn't allow myself to enjoy this person who'd stumbled into my life.

I drove to Fayetteville, to Kinko's on North College. In front of the building in a dispenser, the local paper said Milton's killers were still at large. Also, another elk had been found dead. A copycat killing, the authorities said.

From a pay phone I called the newspaper in Triple Oaks, West Virginia, asked if they could fax me a picture of Helen Spangler and a copy of the story.

"Do you have information about her?" the voice on the phone said.

"Don't know yet," I said. "Send the fax."

"Can you call back and confirm? This is a big deal here."

"Sure," I said. I hung, up and stood there for a few seconds. I glanced at the fax machine, cold and mechanical behind the counter. I couldn't take it. I didn't want to know. Outside, I climbed back in the truck and drove away.

Her car was gone when I got home. I sat in the truck for several minutes, staring at the house. I was afraid to go inside, afraid there'd be none of her things, no note, no trace of her anywhere. Finally, I climbed out and went in. A note was on the bar, folded under a newly-opened Maker's Mark bottle that was a quarter empty. Seeing the note didn't make me feel any better.

After taking a breath to steady my hands, I unfolded it.

Frank,

I wasn't prepared to meet someone like you. What I wanted wasn't to fall in love. I'm not ready to handle it. It is hard for me to leave this way, but I have to. I've brought you my tragedy. Remember that I do love you, no matter what you may decide about me. I have to keep moving now, but I know I'll never find myself in this predicament again. I will always think of you instead.

Love,
Margot

I read it dozens of times, at first with anger, then with hurt, then longing, then regret that I'd left her alone. Then suspicion and curiosity set in. I called Kinko's and, after explaining I had to take off, asked them to overnight the fax to me. I paid with my credit card over the phone.

That night, sleep would only come with bourbon. The next day I paced the house, waiting for the mail, which usually arrived between one and two. When the Chevy Citation stopped along the road, and the man placed two letters inside the box, I was out the front door, nearly to my box before he'd pulled away. He waved, and I flicked a wave back and grabbed the letters—a Christmas card from my ex-in-laws and an envelope from Kinko's. I carried them inside and sat down, my hands sweating against the paper.

I stared at the letter for a while but didn't open it. I read Margot's note again, trying to find a lie or anything in it to make me want to get back at her. But I couldn't doubt her love, even if I could doubt she was really Margot Bailey. After folding her note and slipping it back into my shirt pocket, I laid the Kinkos envelope on the end table and stood up and made a drink. As I sipped, I looked at the envelope. What if she were Helen Spangler? Could I turn her in? I'd let Harris get away. Could I do it again?

Outside, the dogs started barking and a car pulled in the drive. Thinking it was Margot and wondering how many more of her disappearing/reappearing acts I could take, I ran to the door but saw the Newton County sheriff's Bronco. He climbed out, walked up to the porch. "Mr. Powell," he said, nodding at me.

"Sheriff," I said.

"Mind if I come in?"

I stepped from the doorway and gestured toward the living room.

Inside, he sat on the couch beside the envelope and said, "Been quite a week for you, ain't it?"

"I've had better." I picked up my drink. "Drink?" I asked.

"It's a dry county."

I killed the drink.

"That boy works for you, he ain't been around this week, has he?"

"He quit."

"Quit? How come?"

I made another drink, swallowed hard, and stared outside.

"Needed steadier work, I guess."

"Well, he's a suspect," he said. "He's got a history of such things."

From the corner of my eye I could see him watching me. I glanced at the envelope. "You think it could of been him that shot Milton?" he asked.

"It was dark," I said. "It could've been anybody."

"You couldn't recognize him for sure?"

I looked at him for a few seconds. "I don't know, sheriff. It all happened so fast. I guess it doesn't look good for him since he hasn't shown up for work."

"Nope," he said. "It don't." He watched me a moment longer then stood. "Well, I reckon I've taken up enough of your time," he said. "If you can remember anything, anything at all, you let me know."

"I will," I said.

"Sorry you had to go through that," he said. "Old Milton was a good one."

"He was," I said.

He headed for the door, then stopped. "Oh yeah, one other thing," he said. "Who was that gal that was hanging around here?"

"A stranger," I said, glancing at the letter. "She was just passing through."

"Word had it y'all was getting awful tight."

"Just a fling," I said.

He opened the door. "Get rid of that booze," he said before leaving.

"I plan on it."

He walked out, climbed in his truck, backed out of the drive, then drove away.

I sat on a barstool and finished my drink. Staring at the envelope, I pressed my tongue against the roof of my mouth and tightened my lips to keep them from trembling. Once something started, the rest of me would shake loose. The afternoon light began to fade. I stood, opened the stove door, put a couple of logs on the fire. They flamed up a little. I grasped the envelope, held it for several minutes while watching the flames. I tossed it inside, watched it flare up, its edges turning black and curling. Soon it was a thin black ember, all the words and pictures and truth turned to ash.

Kevin Stewart is a native of Princeton, WV, and a graduate of the University of Arkansas' MFA Programs in Creative Writing. He also holds degrees in English from Radford University, VA, and Concord College, WV, and degrees in Architectural and Civil Engineering from Bluefield State College, WV. After several years of working in architecture, engineering, and auto upholstery and serving as an adjunct instructor, he's a full-time instructor of writing and literature at Louisiana State University. Recently, he has won *Kestrel*'s 1999 Short Story Contest and *Now and Then*'s 1999 Appalachian Fiction Competition, along with the 1997 Elizabeth Simpson Smith Fiction Award for North and South Carolina Writers, a 1997 South Carolina Academy of Authors Fellowship for Fiction, and a 1992 West Virginia Commission on the Arts and Humanities Award for Literature. His fiction has appeared in *The Antietam Review*, *The Distillery: Artistic Spirits of the South*, *Kestrel: A Journal of Art and Literature*, *Now and Then*, *Wind Magazine*, and several other journals.